The Chick and the Duckling

Translated from the Russian of V. Suteyev

by Mirra Ginsburg
Pictures by Jose Aruego & Ariane Dewey

Aladdin Books
Macmillan Publishing Company
New York

Aladdin Books
Macmillan Publishing Company
866 Third Avenue, New York, NY 10022
Collier Macmillan Canada, Inc.

First Aladdin Books edition 1988

Printed in the United States of America

A hardcover edition of *The Chick and the Duckling* is
available from Macmillan Publishing Company.

10   9   8   7

to Libby

A Duckling came out
of the shell.

"I am out!" he said.

"Me too," said the Chick.

"I am taking a walk,"
said the Duckling.

"Me too,"
said the Chick.

"I am digging a hole,"
said the Duckling.

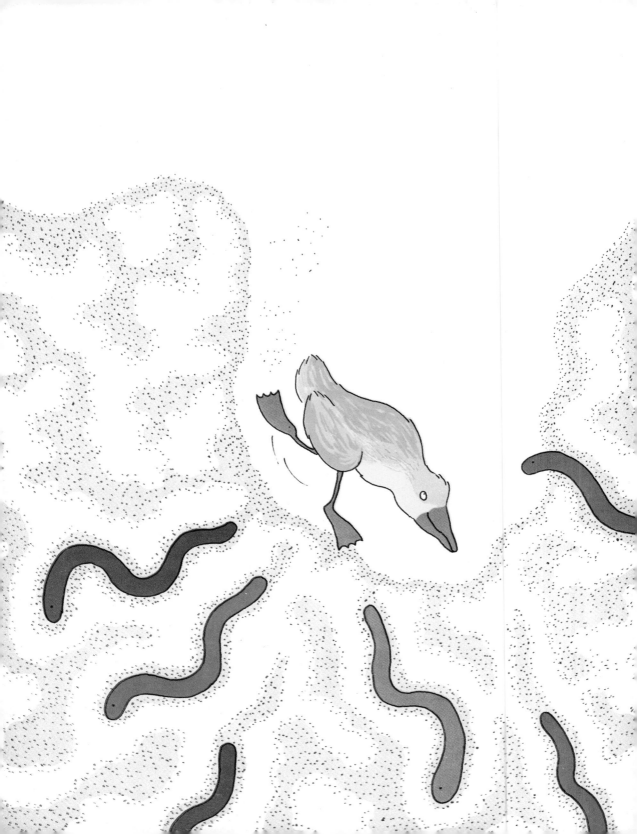

"Me too,"
said the Chick.

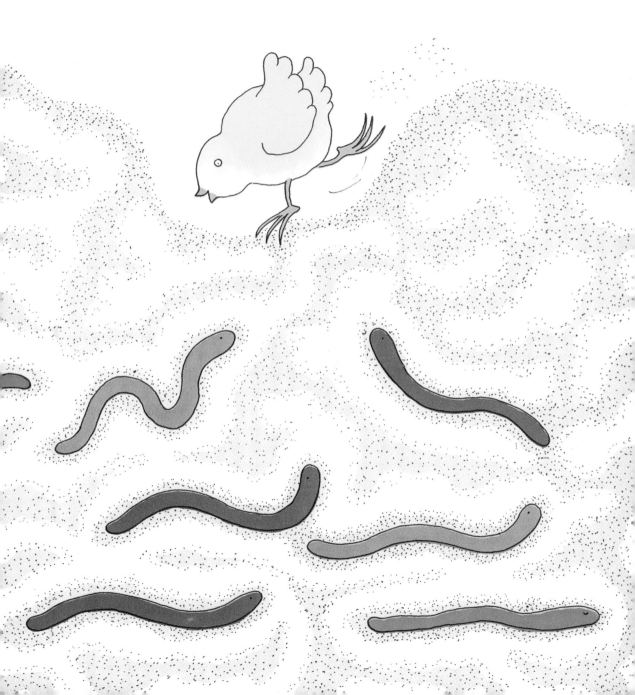

"I found a worm,"
said the Duckling.

"Me too,"
said the Chick.

"I caught
a butterfly,"
said the
Duckling.

"Me too,"
said the Chick.

"I am going for a swim,"
said the Duckling.

"Me too," said the Chick.

"I am swimming,"
said the Duckling.

"Me too!"
cried the Chick.

The Duckling pulled the Chick out.

"I'm going for another swim,"
said the Duckling.

"Not me,"
said the Chick.